Journal of a Schoolyard Bully

Journal of a Schoolyard Bully

Notes on Noogies, Wet Willies, and Wedgies

Farley Katz

St. Martin's Griffin

New York

JOURNAL OF A SCHOOLYARD BULLY. Copyright © 2011 by Farley Katz. All rights reserved. Printed in the United States of America. For information, address St. Martin's Press, 175 Fifth Avenue, New York, N.Y. 10010.

www.stmartins.com

ISBN 978-0-312-68158-6

First Edition: September 2011

Printed in July 2011 in the United States of America by RR Donnelley, Harrisonburg, Virginia

10 9 8 7 6 5 4 3 2 1

Journal of a Schoolyard Bully

Dear Journal,

God, that sounds stupid.

Bully's Log. Monday. 21:00.

That's better. Sounds tougher at least. No
matter how I write this thing, I just know this
is going to turn up on YouTube in like five years
and embarrass me worse than that tiger who
got sleepy and fell into that swimming pool full
of toothpaste.
    Side note: If I were old enough for a tattoo,
I'd get this on my neck:

Tuesday

Well, here we go again. Round two. Author's note: I am being forced to write this as part of an exercise to find out "why I behave the way I do." Dr. Shaeffer says I have to keep a journal to do this. He thinks I bully kids because of my "fear of disappointing my father." Am I really supposed to listen to a grown man who plays with puppets?

The real reason I bully kids is because I'm good at it—no, I'm **great** at it. It is my calling, my reason for being.

Charles Darwin will tell you that fish crawled out of the primordial waters, grew legs, turned into monkeys, and then eventually turned into nerds like him. What he forgot was the all-important final stage in evolution: bullies.

You see, nerds and bullies aren't all too different from one another—they both have their problems. The difference is a bully isn't afraid to stand up and do something about it. Something reckless.

Wednesday

Dr. Shaeffer says writing down my thoughts is supposed to help me learn to "be happy with myself." That sounds super dumb, but Dr. Shaeffer did go to grad school for fifteen years, so that had to be good for something, right?

I Googled Dr. Shaeffer and found some pretty funny pictures of him. He used to have real long hair and liked to drink adult sodas.

NYE 1976

Well, technically it's not only Dr. Shaeffer who's making me write this journal. It's part him, part my mom, and part Vice Principal Jones. Aka "the Unholy Trinity."

They decided it was time to do something after the incident last month. You see, grade A. wimp Eugene Steiner was really getting on my nerves, so I did what any logical, rational seventh grader would do.

Remember, kids—toilet water is only safe for dogs and dorks.

Dr. Shaeffer always asks me if I feel sorry for what I've done. Usually I just tell him what he wants to hear.

Honestly, I'm not sorry. Not one stinking bit. Eugene had it coming to him when he decided it was OK to look me in the eye. He may not have said anything—he didn't need to—I knew what he was **thinking.**

"Sorry" isn't the word for how I feel ... it's more like ... "unrepentant," "remorseless," or "impenitent." Man, I never thought this thesaurus would be good for anything besides its primary use.

Actually, all I feel right now is <u>hungry</u>.
Time for a hot dog break.

Friday

Oh boy. I'm panicking. I just did something so bad that when Vice Principal Jones finds out, I think his head might explode.

There was no way I could possibly go to school and face Jones, so I faked sick. All I had to do was make up a batch of fake vomit (oatmeal and green food coloring) and wait for my mom to come wake me up. I deserve an Oscar for my acting abilities.

But I was so anxious about getting caught that I could barely enjoy my precious daytime television shows.

Normally I love this kind of stuff. Not to mention the unlimited video games and high-fructose carbonated corn drink (Mom says it's the same as soda but half the price).

If V.P. Jones finds out what I did, he's going to do to me what Dr. MurderGun does to everyone. (He murders them, duh.)

Well, while I'm stuck at home "sick" and unable to enjoy myself, I might as well get down some of my bullying philosophy—you know, to save the historians and bullyologists time later.

Nicknames

Picking a mean-spirited nickname to call someone is a delicate process best left to seasoned bullies. It is essential to choose a nickname that is both demeaning—so the kid knows you mean business—and catchy—so that other kids won't forget it.

Here are some examples of good nicknames coined by yours truly:

Peter Dane, aka Peter Danish, aka Peter Poundcake, aka Peter Peter Poly-saturated Fats Eater

Because he is overweight, these nicknames draw attention to his physical differences. Simple, but effective. I know this because once in the first grade Brett March called me "Professor Fat Guy." I haven't seen Brett in a long time. I wonder if he's still in that hole I buried him in.

14

Rachel Delaney, aka Rachel "Snot-head" Delaney
An obvious choice would have been Rachel

complainy (on account of how she is always complaining about things), but I think the "Snot-head" touch adds an element of the unexpected. She sits in front of me in history class, and her hair smells like peaches.

Marvin Rooney, aka Loser-pants McGeek, aka the Weinermobile, aka Dweeb-bot 3000

Marvin always gets A's without even trying. These nicknames are the price he pays.

Fred Peekman, aka Dead Fred

Fred crossed me severely when he asked me in front of the whole class why my dad doesn't live with me. Now Fred has to live with weekly wedgies.

Monday
Unfortunately, Mom didn't buy the sick ruse for a second time.

As soon as I got to school I realized that the crime had been uncovered but a suspect had not yet been apprehended.

I forced half the kids to take pro and half to take con. The cons just wanted it more, I guess. Genius, I know. Seeing my work in print was even sweeter than doing the deed itself. That was until Jones decided to round up the suspects.

I know from <u>Law & Order</u> that it's best to remain silent during questioning and wait for an attorney, but what do they really have on me anyway? I usually leave my calling card at the scene of a crime. Luckily at the time of this particular crime, I was all out and the new cards were still being processed at the printers due to a typo.

NIKO KAYLER
—professional bully—

specializing in beat-ups, hit-downs, insults, general punches, nerd-kissing

crushing! It's supposed to read "crushing"!

And then, in an M. Night Shyamalan twist, Little Lucy, the school's second most feared bully and goth girl extraordinaire, did something unexpected.

This tells us two important things. One, that Little Lucy is not a real bully. No self-respecting nerd pummeler would take credit for someone else's work. And two, that sometimes it pays to work in the vicinity of crazy people.

Wednesday

I thought I was in the clear with the whole debate incident. I had even begun planning my next big move.

The script basically wrote itself.

There's nothing lower than a snitch. And, apparently, the debate team is made up entirely of snitches. Even though Little Lucy was doing time in detention hall, taking the heat for me and simultaneously fulfilling her need for punishment (that'll manifest itself in fun ways later in her life, I bet), the team decided to stand up for themselves and squealed on me.

When they hauled me in, there wasn't exactly a welcoming party waiting. Inside V.P. Jones's den of misery sat the Unholy Trinity assembled, and nobody was smiling.

In these kinds of situations, where you are faced with an unfriendly crowd, I find it's best to open with a joke.

But sometimes, even a hilarious tidbit of observation humor won't win over the enemy.

The debate team torture incident was repeatedly referred to as "strike seven" and "the last straw" by Jones, "an unforgivable disaster" by my mom, and "the result of lashing out at his own insecurities and weight issues" by Dr. Shaeffer. Note to self: Make Shaeffer pay for that.

They came to the dramatic conclusion that:

One more bullying incident, and Niko Kayler will be permanently expelled from checkers Nixon Memorial Middle School forever and ever until the end of time, so help me DOG!

(I think he meant to say "God," but Jones is a touch dyslexic and tends to slip a little when worked up.)

I've been slapped on the wrist before—heck, I've even been reprimanded—but this seemed like the threat of an actual **punishment**. I looked to Mom and Doctor Shaeffer—Wildman Jones was obviously on a power trip, making nutso outlandish threats—

but surely <u>they</u> would support me?

I guess this time I'm really on my own.

Friday

Things were looking bad for your humble narrator. Two days had passed and Jones's threat seemed to be standing. Sure, Jones talked the talk, but would he walk the walk? Would his bite be as big as his bark? Would his booger be as big as his nose?

Well, I wasn't about to test him and find out, most especially when the threat was so fresh. Don't get me wrong, it's not like I love checkers Nixon Memorial. It's a stupid school with a stupid mascot.

Yes, that's right, our school mascot is
one of the most feared creatures of all
the jungle, a terrifying elephant named
"Daisy." (That's what happens when you let
a group of second-grade girls name the
mascot.)

But after one and a half years, I'm
used to it here. I'm a big bully-shark in
a small pond full of tiny weiner-fish. I
don't know what lies outside the walls of
Checkers Nixon, and I don't care to find
out. I guess for now, I'll have to keep the
bullying to a philosophical level.

Intimidation

The key to striking fear into the hearts of nerds and dweebs alike is managing your expression of anger. You must control your outward show of anger to properly harness it. Here's what I mean.

Threat level Green

As a bully, it's important to always maintain a veneer of slight anger and frustration, even when everything is OK—this is how people will know you're a bully.

Threat level Yellow

I resort to this level of alertness when confronted with normal, everyday annoyances like when a nerd drops his pencil, or when someone coughs, or even for minor pests of nature like happy songbirds and playful kittens.

Threat level Orange

This is how you let the people know you mean business. If you hold your breath and bite your tongue hard enough, you can actually drive steam out of your ear canals. It's true: I saw it on Animal Planet.

Threat level T-Rex

Ok, someone just ate a bite of your lunch by mistake. It's time to bring the fireworks. Channel nature's all-time greatest bully, the tyrannosaur, and let the dino do what he may.

Threat level Black

Reserved for the most severe infractions, like the time Marvin Rooney pointed out that I mispronounced the word "rendezvous" (I'm not stupid, I just refuse to acknowledge the French). A note to all you nerds: If ever you spy a bully with a smile on his face, run for the hills because something terrible is about to go down.

Monday

What do you like to do on the weekend? Do you like to relax and watch TV? How about going to the park and playing with a slobbery dog? Me too! I love that kind of stuff. I live for it. In fact, I would be content spending my entire life's worth of weekends doing things like that. However, things I do NOT like to do on the weekend include spending the entire time boarded up inside of a psychiatrist's office listening to a "doctor" yak on and on about the best ways to change the essence of who I am.

Shaeffer and Mom decided I should spend two days being broken down by a grown man who still sleeps alone in a twin bed. Here's the ugly recap. Spoiler alert: It sucked.

Hours one through five were spent in denial.

this isn't happening. I feel fine. Nothing wrong here.

Then came anger.

Eventually, I succumbed to bargaining.

That was followed by intense depression.

Finally, after all the ugliness of the previous forty or so hours, came acceptance.

Actually, I just figured out at some point (around hour thirty-nine and a half) that this was the kind of garbage Shaeffer wanted to hear, and the only thing that was going to get me out of there and back to what really mattered: television.

Tuesday

Sometimes, when I'm feeling down, I find it helps to think back on happier times—times when I was on top of my game, when I could bully to my heart's content without the constant threat of being expelled.

My greatest hits include the sixth-grade winter formal. Everybody always looks forward to these stupid boy-girl dances, so I decided to give them something they could really look forward to: living the rest of their lives with an incurable case of cooties!

THE COOTIES PANDEMIC

1999 —A Handful of cases

Today —Thousands Infected Globally

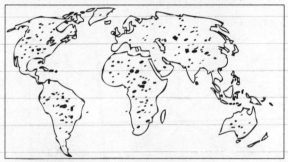

2015 —Entire World Has Cooties

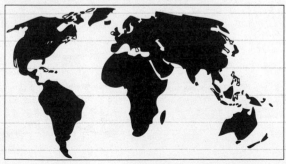

By volunteering to work the front desk at the dance, I both got time taken off my after-school detention sentence (only four hundred and fifteen days left!) AND got access to the dance's raffle tickets, which I handed out along with a dollop of Super Glue, aka "prank sauce."

During the first slow dance, the glue went to work, making sure any of the kids stupid enough to be dancing with each other would stay dancing with each other for the indefinite future.

And then there was the sixth-grade science fair, or "Nerd Christmas," as they call it. But, this christmas, Santa was bringing something far worse than coal: teenagers looking to party!

I papered the local bars and teen hangouts with this flyer:

Battle of the Bands.

Free beer!

Local bands welcome to perform. No dumb adults to ruin rebellious fun.

Checkers Nixon Memorial Middle School gym, 6 p.m.

The result was memorable enough to get a mention in the local news.

"Hundreds of local teens in search of a 'good time' turned checkers Nixon Middle School's science fair into a rowdy rock-and-roll alcohol concert. Sadly, all the science projects were destroyed."

And who could forget the fifth-grade science fair?

"A swarm of killer bees ruined an area science fair when a mysterious giant barrel of honey was dumped into the gym. Police and apiarists are baffled."

come to think of it, I've rained down havoc on the yearly science fair for as long as I can remember. It's basically a tradition. Looks like this year they'll finally be able to enjoy themselves and their lame egg-drop "experiments." Just thinking about it makes me sick.

One day mankind will harness this technology not for eggs, but for humans! Or, barring that, bigger eggs, I suppose.

Thursday

Well, it's been a weird week. I have somehow managed to restrain the inner bully for fear of Jones following through on what he said. I did have one close call, though.

And now to bend down and tie my shoe. I sure hope no one gives me a wedgie. I'm wearing my extra stretchy spandex underwear that would be perfect for that kind of thing. Also, today is my birthday, so that would really be a bonus for the bully doing it.

I had to behave, because everywhere I went, Jones wasn't far behind. It's like he has a tracking device on me or something.

    It's really bad, because Jones seems so intent on enforcing this ridiculous ban on bullying. Worse still, it seems my not bullying has rubbed off on the lesser bullies and made them stop bullying, too. I even spotted Little Lucy this week volunteering for hall monitor duty—a nerd's job! Disgusting!

Does Jones realize what he is doing? Has he even stopped to consider the consequences of his actions? What would happen in a world without bullies? It would be mayhem. Without bullies, nerds would have no one to keep them in line. They'd become like **GODS**, ruling over the student body with a nerdy iron fist. The gym and cafeteria would be converted into libraries and jock detention centers. It would be a horrible dystopia where science and math ruled, where everyone had four eyes.

And the worst part of all is that I'm only in seventh grade. Not only do I have to continue behaving like a saint for the rest of this year, but for another entire year after that. And that, my friends, is impossible.

Monday

Shame on you for thinking I did this! First of all, I would never sink so low as to degrade myself in order to bully others. Second of all, I'm supposed to be on good behavior and have somehow managed to do that for nearly a week now. The lowbrow bullying headline you see there is the work of the beefy bully named Biff. His highlight reel includes:

* CHECKERS NIXON REPORTER *

KID FORCES OTHER KID TO PICK, EAT BOOGERS.

He's kind of a one-trick pony. The guy could really use some new material, and I might be just the one to give it to him.

Wednesday
It's becoming painfully clear that I'm not going to be able to quit bullying cold turkey.

Last night I woke up shaking in pool of sweat, delirious from bully withdrawal.

As the school's alpha bully, I hold great influence over the other lesser bullies. I say, "Punch," and they say, "How hard?" I decided to use this sway to get my bully jollies by proxy. To you laymen, that means I will bully through other bullies, kind of like Avatar, but with bullies.

Step 1. Select a target. Since I had been dreaming of Fred Peekman, I figured why argue with my subconscious? Plus, I'd been itching to get this guy for a while.

Step 2. Formulate a plan. Two things I know about Fred: 1. He's lightweight, like a bird with hollow bones. 2. He has a devastating fear of heights.

Step 3. Select a venue. The weekly school assembly gives the teachers and administrators a chance to address the student body. It gives bullies the perfect staging ground for a large-scale public prank.

Step 4. Select an Avatar. This prank was not a high-level thinking man's kind of prank, so Biff would be the perfect fall guy for the job. Plus, with his recent booger busts, Jones was probably itching to put him away for good. More important, Biff, twice left behind a grade, has the build of an adult with a five o'clock shadow, and with the right costume, he can easily pass for a construction worker.

Step 5. Execute. After some subtle whisperings into Biff's ear, he was thoroughly convinced that Fred Peekman was out to get him.

"I heard Fred saying something bad about you."
"Me angry! Me want hurt boy what say bad thing!"
"That can be arranged."

I made sure to get a prime seat where I could watch the action unfold. As the assembly started up, and Jones started to yammer on and on about this or that, no one noticed Biff banging around in the beams above them. For one thing, construction workers had been busy "remodeling" the place for the past decade or so. And they didn't notice anything out of place about Biff, who fit in perfectly in his construction worker costume provided by yours truly.

No one noticed anything out of the ordinary until a conspicuous construction hook lowered itself conveniently down to the seat of Fred Peekman's pants. Biff may not be good at math or talking or much else, but the kid has good aim. Once the hook was securely in place under Fred's belt loop, up he went, like a nerdy rainbow trout being reeled in by a big, apelike fisherman.

Once he reached a safe yet terrifying height, I instructed Biff to fasten him to the overhead fans, creating a lovely spinning mobile not unlike something from Cirque du Soleil. What? Just because I'm a bully, I can't be cultured?

At this point, it was important for kids sitting in the splash zone to put on their rain ponchos and goggles. Because as anyone who's afraid of heights knows, exposure to them can often lead to tears.

Thursday
Isn't it great when things work out the way you planned?

Of course, I didn't mean for the guy to get expelled, but then again, I didn't NOT mean for him to get expelled. This is too much fun to stop now.

Practice Makes Perfect

The key to being perceived as a bully is practice. When you're out there in the schoolyard doing bully stuff, the last thing you want is to come off as an amateur. To avoid this, you've got to practice your bullying routines off of the schoolyard. Perfect them before the main event.

My practice subject of choice is my little brother, Alex. He's supersmart and interested in nerdy things like books and Internet. Thus, he is the perfect person to test out my new bully stuff on.

After years of bullying, Alex probably doesn't like me much. Actually, I know that for a fact. Earlier this week . . .

You know, Niko, after years of bullying, I don't like you much.

And even though that's the case, I was willing to bet that he still would care about me enough to worry if he accidentally caused my death. All I needed was a skateboard and a bottle of ketchup.

I know that every day after school, Alex runs to his room to do his homework. But every day, right around 4:13 p.m., his stomach gets the better of him.

This is right about when Alex comes bounding
out of his room and around the corner to the
stairs. This is also when a string attached
to the outside of his door handle activates a
prerecorded distress call via my phone.

A well-placed, wheels-spinning skateboard and some artfully done ketchup makeup and the little guy is sure he's killed his only brother.

And then comes the big reveal.

He never thinks my pranks are as hilarious as I do.

Friday

Two days have passed since my successful proxy bully, and I'm still seeing the benefits. Why quit when you're ahead? That would be like sitting at a roulette table and NOT betting on black: just plain ig'nant.

My next target was someone I'd been
itching to get for a while, Rachel Delaney.
She loaned me a pencil once in history
class, causing Colin Sykes to do this:

Oooooh! Rachel and *Niko* sitting in a tree, K-I-S-S...

Someone found himself sitting in a tree, but it wasn't me. Did you know that the tallest tree in the world is located right here in the U.S. of A.? It's a coastal redwood, known to nerds as sequoia sempervirens. It stands an imposing 379.3 feet and is only a short drive away, in Redwood National Park, California. I bet Colin Sykes knows this better than anyone.

The no clothes bit was a nice touch, no?

Anyway, I didn't want people to think that just because I took Rachel's pencil, and that I sit behind her in several classes, and that her skin is as silky and smooth as one million thread count Egyptian cotton bedsheets, meant that I—gag—wanted to be K-I-S-S-I-N-G her in a tree or anywhere else! Also, I thought if the bullying I gave her was clever enough, maybe she would notice and appreciate it?

Today being Valentine's Day, every girl's favorite day, it was the perfect opportunity for such a prank. Here at Checkers Nixon Memorial, Valentine's Day is a way for the school to make a million bucks off selling carnations. No one has ever sent me one, and thank goodness, because if they did, I'd be indirectly funding V.P. Jones's terrorist voodoo activities.

Niko, Niko, a curse I speak-o!

So I figured, if girls like carnations, maybe Rachel would enjoy the carnation's distant relative, the rare South African death weed.

Scientists have described the death weed's fragrance as "that of a rotting zebra carcass," "unbreathable," and "worse than a fat guy's burrito fart." The leaves are razor sharp, and a casual touch can result in the equivalent of one million paper cuts. In the summer months, its stamens vibrate, causing an extremely high-pitched and unpleasant ringing known to have deafened thousands of South Africans. If the pollen is ingested, your head swells up to the size of a watermelon before popping like a horrible brain zit. Gross, I know.

But that isn't the only gift
Rachel would receive for Valentine's
Day. She'd also get a large box of
chocolate-covered bugs, both courtesy
of this week's proxy bully, Little Lucy.

No one would question girl-on-girl bullying involving candies and flowers on Valentine's Day. I simply signed the cards "Love, Lucy" and let Jones do the rest.

Again, the best part was watching someone else take the fall. Ah, the perfect crime. The whole thing was wrapped up in one nifty little package. That is, until the end of history class, when the carnations were delivered.

Sometimes, being a bully isn't easy. You've got to have a titanium exoskeleton and a heart of black steel. You can't let anything stand between you and your mission.

The Bully's Creed

Neither snow, nor rain, nor heat, nor gloom of night
Shall stop us bullies from instilling fright
In nerds and wimps, and adults with no spine,
'Tis our solemn bully duty to make you whine.

For wherever there's a weiner without a tormentor,
A shiny new car with an undented fender,
A nerdy science whiz who got an A plus plus,
Or a girl who's never seen a wound full of puss,
A bully shall be there to right these wrongs
Raining down terror while humming this song.

Monday
Apparently, Jones wasn't the only one tailing
me these last few weeks. It seems Mom had
been keeping a close eye on me, too.

She was there when Peekman got his, but I suspect she didn't have the goods to pin it on me. That wasn't the case with the Rachel incident. Moms have some kind of sixth sense for girl stuff, because as soon as I came home, something told me that she knew.

Now I'm on double-secret triple grounding—
like that means anything—because Mom
wants to punish me but doesn't want Jones
to find out and boot me out of school. Also,
she's forcing me to increase my trips to Dr.
Shaeffer's office. Worst of all, it looks like
my days of proxy bullying are over. Whatever.
This sucks. The world is unfair. Everyone is
stupid and smells like wet gerbils.

Wednesday

Sometimes something good can come from something bad. There I was, being tortured on Dr. Shaeffer's couch, thinking about how I'd rather be doing homework—I know, things had gotten pretty desperate—but then Shaeffer said something that made me think.

I'm not alone! Even though I can't bully my nerds at my school, there are plenty of other schools full of equally good nerds ripe for the bullying. I was so happy I did something rash.

Friday

On my lunch hour today, I decided to do something insane and skip lunch. Don't worry, I'm not trying to slim down in order to become one of those sexy supermodels you see in the magazines—I did it for evil!

Instead of lunch, I took a bus ride across town to the Anthony Bourdain Culinary Middle School for Young Chefs. It's an entire school full of nerdy cooking geeks, perfect for the bullying. All I had to do was look the part.

These kitchen jockeys were about to get a bully panini. I started with the obvious:

Then I moved on to more advanced methods.

Tonight we offer a lovely bacon—wrapped nerd, followed by a Hawaiian luau geek, finished off with a light chocolate "moose." I slay myself.

I even learned a thing or two about cooking while I was at it:

It was as if these kids had never seen a bully before. I guess that's probably because not too many bullies end up in culinary middle school. That is, until now.

Tuesday

Even though bullying at the culinary school is outstanding, it is taking a lot out of me. I love bullying and I would gladly sell my pinkie toes to do it, but taking the crosstown bus at lunchtime only gives me fifteen minutes to inflict discomfort on the cooking school nerds before having to hop back on the bus to get to checkers Nixon in time for fifth period. This commute is killing me! Plus, the bus is full of weird "bus people."

There's got to be a better way! I wonder if I could convince a group of nerds to be homeschooled with me in my house?

Thursday
My bully operations at school had been shut
down by Jones. Avatar bullying unplugged by Mom.
Bullying at the cooking school was just too much
travel to be worth it. So, I was forced to work
from home today.

Even Alex, one of my favorite targets, had
stopped falling for the stunts where I made
him think he'd accidentally killed his own family.

So, I decided for the next prank on little Alex I'd have to think outside the box. I started where every good criminal mastermind begins: craigslist.

craigslist > gigs > talent gigs

Need lady actress who looks exactly like my mom
8:38AM EDT

see pic.

No weirdos!!!

* it's NOT OK to contact this poster with services
* Compensation: 20 big ones

PostingID: 19sdf895

After a number of subpar auditions...

I finally found an almost perfect
doppelgänger for my mom. And for only
twenty bucks, I got her to take Alex on a
car ride.

"Mom, you look a little different than normal."
"How?"
"I don't know. Just different. Since when do you have so many arm tattoos?"
"Do you want to go to the candy store or not!?"
"Of course I do!"
"OK, but before we do, we have to make a pit stop at the doctor."
"I guess it could be worse. Just a routine checkup, right?"
"Well, the doctor's office called and said all your records were lost in a fire. Now we have to go back in and get you all new shots for every one of the diseases you've been immunized for over the years. Also, the fire burned all the small needles they usually use for kids and all they have left are the giant needles they use on rhinos. They're as thick as soda straws!"

By the time they got to the doctor's office,
Alex was a shivering wreck, and it was time
for my favorite part of any well-executed
bullying: the rubbing in the face.

Ah, that feels good. That should buy me
a few more days of rest before I have to
strike again. Sometimes I feel like a vampire
who needs to feed, except instead of blood,
I feed on the tears of nerds. Also, I can go
outside during the daytime. And I don't have
any superpowers except for superstrength and
my ability to get sent to the principal's office
a shocking number of times per week.

cyberbullying

Text messages, Facebook, and online boards have made it supereasy for any Joe Laptop or Susie Smartphone to cyberbully without fear of retaliation. Seems like the perfect solution to my problems, right? Nope. I think it's cheap and dirty. Like falling in love in Las Vegas. Or eating food off the ground hours after the five-minute rule is up. I'm not saying I'm above this (my record stands at four hours thirty-six minutes past), but I do think cyberbullying is a poor excuse for an age-old art.

cyberbullying is basically a three-year-old flicking his boogers at you over the Internet. No real bully would sink so low.

Friday

During a particularly boring therapy session with Dr. Shaeffer yesterday, all I could think about was how my bullying days were over. I would either have to defy Jones, bully someone openly, and be expelled from school, or I would have to become "normal" and live like a nerd for the rest of my days. Talk about a suck sandwich.

Then, something amazing occurred to me: Why have I been limiting my bullying to kids my age while I'm surrounded by perfectly good adults in need of bullying? Shaeffer was the ideal test subject.

"Niko, do you see now that many of your problems stem from a desire to please your father, who was absent for much of your youth?"

"Oh, my God, I do!"

"Really?"

"Yes. Dr. S., can I ask you a question?"

"Sure, whatever you want. This has been a big breakthrough!"

"Why does a grown man like yourself not have a family of your own?"

"That's just a choice I made."

"Really? Seems like a funny choice. Did you ever even have a girlfriend?"

"Who needs a girlfriend when you have your books?"

"Can a book hold you at night? Can a book tell you everything's going to be OK? Can a book defend you in front of your so-called friends when they openly mock you at dinner parties <u>you</u> throw for <u>**them**</u>?"

TEN MINUTES LATER

"Shaeffer, do you see now that many of
your problems stem from your inability
to interact socially with others caused by
an extreme case of full-blown adult nerd
syndrome?"

"Oh, my God, you're right."
"And what must you do now?"
"I don't know. For the first time in my life, I honestly don't know."
"The answer is give yourself a wedgie."
"I don't see how that would help."
"Ahem! Who is the doctor here?"

Saturday
After bullying an adult to tears with a few carefully placed words, I decided why stop now?

My next target was Old Man McGee, who runs the corn farm down the street. He's your classic old man who's terrified of the Internet and always yells stuff like:

Should I do my old standby and make him think he killed his entire family? No way! The guy is like a million billion years old and deals with death on a daily basis. The obituaries are basically a high school reunion for him. A few more dead people are no sweat off his liver-spotty back.

To really torture an old man, you have to think like an old man. What do old people hate more than anything? Answer: loud youth music.

I waited until he fell asleep (right around 6 p.m.) before sneaking into his house and installing tiny yet extremely loud remote-controlled headphones inside of his ear canals.

Next came the all-important question of what music to blast down his sound holes. An obvious choice would be heavy metal or noise rock, but again, to bully an old man, you have to think like an old man. What would an old man find most offensive? Probably the sexually subversive hip-gyrating songs of those no-good Beatles, with their long girl haircuts and electronic guitars!

Yeah, that would have been pretty sweet, but that's not what happened. I didn't take into account that the old man has industrial-grade hearing aids in both his ears for what could graciously be called a hearing impairment. The hearing aids must have been so close to the speakers that they blocked all the sound and only sent through a subliminal message.

Rest assured, this will not stand. I will fix this old man and his stupid corns.

Sunday

After yesterday's failure, I needed to regroup. If I couldn't blow up his eardrums, maybe I could break his brain.

Based on dusty photos in his house, before Old Man McGee was a corn farmer, he was a soldier.

Using some carefully placed smoke bombs and props, I would trick his old feeble mind into thinking he was back in the war.

Judging by Old Man McGee's reaction, I think the plan worked.

TiVo back five minutes, before I tricked McGee. To complete this plan, I needed to enlist the help of my brother, Alex. I knew he would never knowingly go along with it, so I preyed on his weakness: McDonald's fries.

Once Alex was safely inside McGee's house, all I had to do was slip a hat on him while he was busy with the fries and let the old man do what our government had trained him to.

Relax! I wasn't about to let the old man get Alex. If anyone is gonna bully my one and only brother, it's gonna be me. The final phase of this plan involved some people I usually consider enemies.

The boys in blue did not disappoint.
Within minutes, Alex was safe, back
eating street fries, and McGee was
being taken to a better place.

Old Men Committed to State Institutions: 1
Brothers Accidentally Murdered in the Process: 0

All in all, I'd say it was a successful day.

Wednesday

After an amazing weekend of out-of-school bullying, things back at Checkers Nixon took a turn for the worse.

Even though bullying the old folks was fun, it just wasn't the same. I felt an overwhelming urge to slap a "Kick Me" sign on a dweeb or poke a nerd in his solar plexus. But, all my school bullying options exhausted, I didn't know what to do. So I did something I never thought I'd have to resort to: I joined a school sports team.

Even though joining something school sponsored is totally lame, football seems pretty close to bullying, at least in theory. You are encouraged to tackle people. The point of the game is to slam your body into the other guys', with the intent to crush as many bones as possible. It is legal to hit someone so hard that his head pops off. Well, I'm not sure about that last one, but it definitely seems like something that could be true.

Anyway, I hope it turns out awesome, because right now, sitting here in these heavy, hot pads, it kind of seems like it's gonna suck.

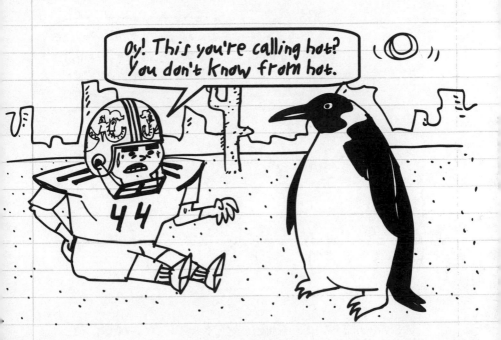

Thursday

After day one, I was a little worried about this whole football thing, but then I met Coach Doug Killman.

Pain is just fear leaving the body, so let's make some pain milkshakes!

The man stands seven feet tall. His neck is thicker than three redwoods. His legs are hairier than a bear's butt! He carries an ear-piercing whistle around his neck that he blows whenever he wants, just to freak kids out. You can see the pleasure in his eyes when he screams at kids to climb up ropes and calls them "wussies" when they can't do enough pull-ups. I've heard tell that he made Timmy Nagler do push-ups until his arms fell off!

And word on the street is, one time after some kids cut gym class, Killman followed them home and made them drink a glass of his sweat! The best part of all is the school actually pays him to do these things (twice as much as Mr. Borchart gets for teaching English!).

I think I've found a new role model. Speaking of role models, I've been compiling a list of important bullies throughout history.

Bullying Hall of Fame
(It's like the Baseball Hall of Fame, except everyone isn't a total ween.)

Genghis Khan
Ruler of the Mongol Empire, on the outside Genghis Khan seems like a boring historical figure. In fact, I first found out about this dude when I had to write a stupid paper on him for sixth-grade history class. Turns out he was awesome! He became an emperor by bullying all his enemies into giving up. Sometimes he'd even eat them! (I don't know if that's true, but I put it in my report to spice things up.) One thing's for sure, he set the bar for bullies being overweight. He used his wide girth to his advantage, sitting on the faces of enemies until they cried uncle. As a fat guy myself, I respect this.

Napoleon Bonaparte

Napoleon was a bully, to compensate for something he was unhappy about: his short stature (and probably the fact that his name was basically "Nip-pole-lion Boner-fart"). Dr. Shaeffer likes to say that I'm a bully "to compensate for my father's absence in my life." Napoleon would probably have made Shaeffer lick the dog drool off his shoe. Like Khan, Napoleon bullied by sheer force and strength, and like Khan, he was someone I had to learn about for a stupid history project.

Garfield

Garfield was a relentless, mean-spirited bully, and a darn good one. Whenever that dumb dog Odie got in his way, what did Garfield do? He shoved him off the table. How about Garfield's lame cousin Nermal? When she got on his nerves, he put her in a box and mailed her to Abu Dhabi. And when Garfield's master, the weak-minded weiner Jon, would make dinner for the two of them, Garfield would gobble down the entire thing and laugh in Jon's face. Garfield's only flaw: He was too lazy to rise to the top. Good bullies never rest until the job is done.

Magneto

So far, all the bullies in the Hall of Fame have
been tough guys—bullies who rule by the fist.
Not Magneto. He was what I like to refer to
as a "brain-bully." He used his smarts and his
wits to bully others with his mind. He managed
to turn a whole group of mutants against the
X-Men, who by all accounts should have been
their besties. He also managed to outsmart
Professor X, who, judging by the size of his big
bald head, is somewhere between a level five
and a level six übernerd. Magneto could have
easily grown up to be a nerd like Professor X
but instead decided to use his smarts for
good (evil). I guess he also had the power of
magnets, which helped. Of the bullies in the
BHF, I relate most to Magneto. He and I would
be twins if only he were fatter and if I could
control metal more.

Lucifer, aka the Devil

The Devil is your classic biblical bully. He was an angel who didn't want to deal with all of God's lame rules, so he decided to pick up, move down south, and do his own thing. Now he spends his days poking people in the butt with pitchforks and his nights thinking up cruel ways to torture sinners for eternity. I envy almost everything about this guy, with the exception of his silly red spandex outfit. I look forward to meeting him in the great beyond.

Santa

Most people would never classify this jolly red giant as a bully, but that's where most people would be wrong. On the happiest day of the year, when kids around the world are getting sweet new bikes and Legos and crap, Santa decides to give kids he doesn't like big chunks of dirty black coal. Sometimes, when he's feeling especially diabolical, he crumples up his list of who's been naughty and who's been nice and gives everyone coal, just because he can! Also, I heard the dude eats kids.

Monday:

The Student Becomes the Master

Today I came home to a horrific crime scene. From the looks of it, someone had broken into my house and ransacked the place.

I went to the kitchen to get the phone and call the cops when I saw something horrible.

In the name of all that is candy, nooooooo!

It seemed Alex Kayler, my one and only brother in all the world, aged ten and two-thirds, had fallen victim to a madman's hurricane of destruction. I cradled his lifeless body in my arms. Is there no justice in the world?

I was so proud. This must be
what it feels like to be a mother.
If Alex can become a full-fledged
bully, one day you can, too.

Certificate of Bullyhood

This is to certify that _____ has forsaken all things nerdy to embrace the dark arts of the bully on this, the _____ day of _____, 20___. In his heart, there is nothing but blood and blackness and maybe some cholesterol from candy.

Signed,

Niko Kayler,
10th Degree Grand Dragon Bully Master

clip and save your
certificate.

Wednesday

Has the world gone crazy? Is up down? Is pee poop? Today when I strolled into math class, it certainly seemed like it. There, in the middle of the room, in front of the whole class was resident sugar behemoth Peter Dane holding hands with the lovely and fair Rachel. Don't get me wrong, she is still a snot-head cootie factory, it's just crazy that she would hold **Peter's** hand!

Does this mean they are girlfriend and boyfriend? Are they going to get married? Do they already have kids?

Aren't we too young to be having girlfriends? I mean, this is only the seventh grade, shouldn't we be "playing the field" or something? Do you think they will name their son "Niko," just to spite me?

The craziest part of all is that Peter is only slightly fatter than I am, and let's be honest, I'm a kid who knows his way around a dessert. If Rachel could like Peter, why wouldn't she like me?!

I don't know what this feeling is. It's stronger than anger, but not quite fury. There's also a hefty dose of Dr. Shaeffer's favorite word, "depression," in there. There's also a touch of hunger (should have packed a hot dog snacker!). I don't know what it is, but I do know what it made me do.

I excused myself to go to the bathroom, but that's not where I went. I went to my special place, my safe zone at Checkers Nixon. The only people who know about it are me and Janitor Jenkins, who doesn't tell on me because we share a common interest.

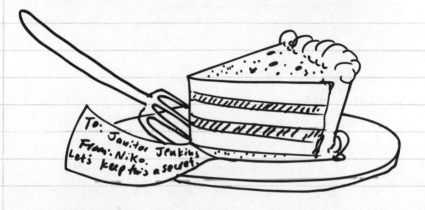

The place I speak of is the rooftop storage shed on the roof above the science wing. I come here when I want to think or just clear my mind, or, more important, I come here to assemble and test weapons of mass bullying destruction.

Automatic Wedgie Machine

One device in particular was perfect for this situation. Lucky for me, my sky lair faced directly across from Mr. Trip's math class, where Peter and Rachel appeared to still be fastened together at the palm.

I call the device the Paper Plane Delivery System. Fully loaded, it can launch six hundred and forty-four paper planes in succession. More important, it has a timer and is self-sustaining, for the bully who can't afford to be caught red-handed at the scene of the crime.

Execute Operation Stink from Above

I set the timer for five minutes. Enough time to allow me to return to class, so as to arouse no suspicion from Mr. Trip. Having synced my watch, I knew exactly the moment when I would need to apply the safety precautions.

Five...four...three...two...six hundred and forty-four paper planes! In groups of twenty or so, they began their steady barrage of Trip's classroom. The first few came unloaded and mostly just poked nerds in the head. A taste of things to come.

The next few wouldn't be so friendly. I had preloaded the jets with materials of different stink grades:

Level 1: Garlic

Level 2: Dead fish

Level 3: Sock sweat

Level 4: Tupperware-encased farts

Level 5: Skunk juice

You may be asking yourself: "Does Niko really catch his farts in Tupperware and have a pet skunk he uses to harness pure stink that he keeps under the house so his mom won't find it?" Yes, yes, a million times yes! And FYI, her name is Princess Smelly.

The planes kept pouring in, and the smells were getting worse. Mr. Trip tried to calm everybody down but eventually crumbled.

It felt good to bully again firsthand. To feel the class tremble beneath me. To see Rachel and Peter's handholding torn apart by my farts.

But deep down in the pit of my stomach, I had a sinking feeling that I would pay for this one.

Thursday

It pained me to watch Jones raid my rooftop lair, destroying years' worth of bully weapons development. Without thinking twice, he threw out the Noogie-namatron, the SBWD (subliminal bed-wetting device), and Weapon Thirteen, the top-secret machine that, once completed, would emit an electronic signal to make all the nerds in the school punch themselves in the face. I was ready to test it but feared Weapon Thirteen was so advanced, it would become self-aware and make all the bullies punch themselves, too.

Even though I had planted evidence to misdirect Jones into thinking Lucy had done the plane stunt, I don't think he took the bait.

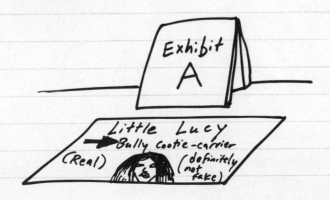

Exhibit
A

Little Lucy
Bully Cootie-carrier

(Real)

(definitely not fake)

Because there I was, hauled back into Jones's office, waiting for my comeuppance. Jones had sworn to kick me out if I slipped up again, and even though my device left no actual evidence to pin this on me, he probably knew I was the only one smart enough and skilled enough to pull off such a feat.

Would Mom kill me when she found out? Almost certainly. In fact, she was probably already in there with Jones, preparing for the deed.

But then, something weird happened. Jones was ... friendly.

"Niko, I heard about what happened in
Mr. Trip's class. Are you OK? I mean, Mr.
Trip said you got stuck in the classroom,
that you were the last one out after the
planes started flying into the room. That
must have been terribly traumatic."

"Uh ... yeah ... I guess so."

"Well, I just wanted to check in on
you and see that you were OK. You know,
your good behavior has not gone unnoticed.
I'm really impressed at how you've been
controlling yourself in class. Marvin
Rooney, your onetime victim, even had nice
things to say about you."

"What! What in the world did that weiner...
I mean ... what did my friend Marvin say?"

"Oh, just that you haven't harassed him at
all for weeks now."

"Crap."

"What?"

"Oh. I said 'rap.' I like rap music."

"Oh. Well, I'll let you get back to class now.
You kids and your rap music!"

And just like that, I was back on the streets.
Defeated. How could Jones not realize that
I am the only one who could have possibly
thought out and executed Operation Stink
from Above?!? Does he think I've gone soft?
And Marvin! He's walking around like a free
man, saying nice things about me? One Halloween
I trapped him inside of a pumpkin and used
him as a bowling ball, and now he's saying "nice
things" about me? I can't take it. My head
is going to explode. I'm about to take this
spaceship full speed to Planet Insanity.

Friday

I decided I needed help, and fast. If I didn't do something soon, I would surely act out again and be expelled by the end of the day.

Help, yes, but not from that marshmallow-eating hippie Shaeffer, but from someone more like me, who could understand where I was coming from.

MTV is good for a lot of things: from its rich variety of documentary shows about young people doing stupid things to its semiscripted "reality" shows about young people doing stupid things. But one thing I saw on MTV did strike home with me: **Scared Straight!**

Scared Straight! is a show where they hire tough-as-nails prisoners to yell in the faces of troubled teens until the teens realize they are on the wrong path and decide to straighten up and stop doing crimes.

I called up the local Scared Straight program and they sent over all six feet seven, three hundred and fifty pounds of a hardened criminal named Razor Blade right to my very home. Seems kinda dangerous sending out an actual prisoner into the world of the free, but they sent along a guard, so what could go wrong?

"YOU THINK CRIME IS COOL!? IT AIN'T! I SPENT HALF MY LIFE BEHIND BARS FOR 'BEING COOL.'"

"Yeah, I guess that sounds pretty bad."

"YOU'RE DARN RIGHT THAT'S BAD! YOU KNOW, I STARTED OUT JUST LIKE YOU. A COCKY LITTLE BULLY WHO THOUGHT BEATING UP KIDS WAS FUN."

"It is."

"WHAT!? DON'T YOU TALK UNTIL I TALK AT YOU!"

"Does that tattoo on your head say 'head'?"

"YEAH, IT'S 'CAUSE I ALWAYS LOSE MY HEAD AND DO STUPID THINGS TO KIDS WHEN THEY ASK TOO MANY QUESTIONS."

"That's good. You should use that as your tagline."

"TAGLINE? DO YOU KNOW WHAT HAPPENS TO YOU IN PRISON SHOWERS?"

"I bet it's a good place to prank the other prisoners. You know, splash them with cold water, make them eat soap, or fill up the showers with sea snakes."

"ACTUALLY, THAT WOULD BE PRETTY FUNNY."

TEN MINUTES LATER

"SO YOU'RE SAYING ALL I HAVE TO DO IS SUBVERT THEIR EXPECTATION OF SECURITY?"

"Exactly, Razor Blade. It seems like you have been listening after all."
"I'VE LEARNED A LOT FROM YOU TODAY. THANK YOU, MR. KAYLER."
"Please, call me Niko."

Needless to say, that did not go as intended, but I did make a friend on the inside, which might come in handy down the road. And before he returned to prison, Razor Blade, or crazy Razey, as he asked me to call him, left me with a touching gift.

Honorary Prisoner Certificate

This is to certify that _Niko Kayler_ has what it takes to do hard time. He may not technically be a felon, but he is in heart and mind, and, God willing, one day he will grace the hallowed halls of cell Block D with his court-mandated presence.

Signed
~~Warden Green~~ Razor Blade

The Prisoner and the Bully: A Scientific Study.
After spending some time with Crazy Razey,
I began to see a lot of similarities between
the life of a bully and the life of a prisoner.
We're not one hundred percent the same, but
we're basically brothers by another mother.

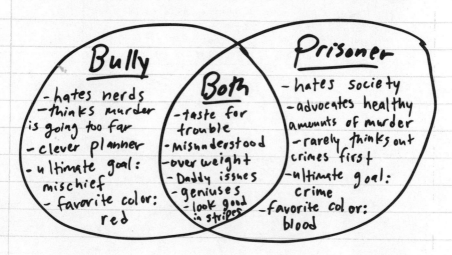

Bully
- hates nerds
- thinks murder is going too far
- clever planner
- ultimate goal: mischief
- favorite color: red

Both
- taste for trouble
- misunderstood
- over weight
- Daddy issues
- geniuses
- look good in stripes

Prisoner
- hates society
- advocates healthy amounts of murder
- rarely thinks out crimes first
- ultimate goal: crime
- favorite color: blood

Monday

Another weekend, another unbearable marathon therapy session with Shaeffer, a man who takes pride in being a grown-up nerd in an unironed, cheez whiz-stained shirt.

Though I've got to say, I appreciated the opportunity to vent, and because of Shaeffer's doctor-patient confidentiality, he couldn't rat me out to Jones.

I did it! I launched the smell planes! I contaminated the classroom so bad, no one can learn in there for years to come! But nobody knows! Is it worth painting a masterpiece if no one will see it? Writing a symphony if no one will hear it? Punching if no nerd will feel it? Dear God, all I want is credit for my genius!

Venting is good, but this is kind of embarrassing. Thank goodness I built a self-destruct device into this journal. If you're a nerd reading this, now would be a good time to get to a bomb shelter.

Wednesday

You've got to believe me when I say I'm trying to behave myself (at least when Jones is looking). Not counting Operation Stink from Above, I've actually done a pretty good job. But when the school posts flyers like this, it makes me think they **WANT** me to rain pain on them.

Checkers Nixon presents:

The 108th Annual Science Fair!

This year's theme: Science as Liberator!

See how science has freed civilization from the oppression of bullies!

Science is my protector!

Attn: scared students and mothers: Don't worry, nothing bad could possibly ever happen this year

I feel like King Kong must have felt when they put those bananas on the Empire State Building.

Monday

It's been an entire week and not a single meltdown. The combination of talking with crazy Razey and yelling at Shaeffer seems to have defused the bomb, at least for now. I just hope I keep things cool until after the science fair.

This is not to say that the week has gone by without incident. I didn't technically bully anyone, but I did do a few things that a meganerd might lump into the category of "bullying."

I don't count things done to Mr. Trip, since he is an adult. Well, sort of. Something you should know about Trip is that he is a young man but is already balding, and he's fighting it hard. He even buys imported Taiwanese hair tonic off the Internet to slow the retreat of his hairline. He has to use it twice a day or he'll be bald by dinnertime.

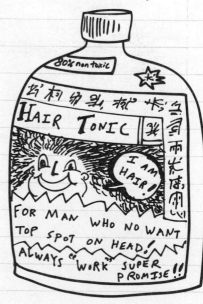

80% non toxic

HAIR TONIC

I AM HAIR!

FOR MAN WHO NO WANT TOP SPOT ON HEAD! ALWAYS "WORK" SUPER PROMISE!!

I may have emptied his hair tonic
bottle and filled it with a drain-unclogging
chemical designed to eat away at hair. I
also may have switched his stomach pills
with Grandpa's sleepy-time pain medicine.
The combo wasn't pretty.

You kids are all right.
I love you guys. Why
don't we hang out more?
Can somebody call Mr.
Hospital?

Don't worry, he'll be fine, but his hair
probably won't. Serves him right for just
sitting there while pudgy Peter Danish held
hands with my Rachel.
I also may have killed someone. Relax, it
was just my imaginary friend, Carlos.

Carlos and I go way back.

But I needed to take out my fury without doing it at school and getting busted. So I attacked carlos with a bowling pin.

But I went too far and did something I regret.

Carlos will be missed.

Princess Smelly, Queen of My Heart

You know what the best thing about having a secret pet skunk is? Everything! It's like a big, stinky dog who will never turn her back on you.

When you're feeling down, there she is, to curl up in a little stinky ball and comfort you.

Why are you the only one who loves me, Princess Smelly?

Skunks are also supersmart, like smelly land dolphins, and can be trained to do tons of awesome stuff.

I guess the downside is that when you have a pet skunk, you get pretty stinky. That's probably why the kids at school are always saying under their breath how bad I smell. I don't care, though. I'm used to it. Even Dr. Shaeffer couldn't help noticing.

Most people who keep pet skunks have the stink glands removed. Not me. I'm a purist. I don't tinker with nature. Plus, without her stink glands, she'd just be a supersmart, stinkless cat.

Tuesday
Football season is in full swing. And for the past few weeks, coach Killman has really been training us hard.

Run like your life depends on it, because it does!

There's nothing like the feeling of a Friday night football game. The crisp grass beneath your cleats. The cool breeze on your brow. The hard crunch of kid bones when you slam into your opponent at ninety miles an hour, like a bully freight train burning uranium in the coal car!

Can you believe this is actually a sport, along with other sports like golf and tennis? Seems to me that football is closer to things that crazy Razey did in his heyday than a sport. Doesn't matter, because right now, this is the best.

I think I've found my new career.

Wednesday

Apparently, if you leave a nerd to his own devices for too long, he gets cocky. Because today Marvin Rooney decided to walk right up to me, in the middle of lunch, with no fewer than thirty other kids sucking down their milk cartons in earshot, to deliver a friendly declaration of war:

> Hey, Niko, do you want to be my partner for the science fair?

In the blink of an eye, the raucous lunchroom fell silent. Straws stopped slurping, forks and spoons were dropped, and somebody even pulled a record needle across a record that was playing for some reason.

Some kind of prehistoric bully reflex
inside of me forced my fingers to curl into
a fist and my arm to cock back into punch
position. The blood drained from Marvin's
face until it went from pink, to pale white,
to a translucent clear. Out of the corner
of my eye I saw Jones, standing there, a
growing grin creeping across his smug face
as he waited to watch what he'd wanted
for so long. He knew this would be it, and he
wanted to savor it.

My fist was seconds away from launching, but I didn't want to go out like this, with Jones sitting front row center at my funeral. I had to think fast. Something important shaeffer said came back to me.

No, not that!

So I aborted the punch sequence. And then, like an idiot, I took Shaeffer's advice and used my words.

"No! I can't be your science partner, Marvin."

"Why not?"

"Uh...because...because I already entered the science fair on my own."

Never lie under pressure. Always premeditate an excuse ahead of time. I knew from the explosive laughter that followed exactly how dumb I sounded. If that wasn't embarrassing enough, Jones decided to rub it in my face.

Oh, Niko, you entered the science fair? You know you have to actually do science, right? It can't just be a project about foods you like.

We have liftoff. In an instant my fist re-formed and blasted off, causing the lunchroom laughter to turn into a collective gasp as my punch rocketed toward Jones. His mouth twisted into a hateful grin—this was just what he wanted. But I refused to give him the satisfaction. Harnessing everything inside of me, I somehow managed to curve the trajectory of my fist sideways, but I couldn't stop it completely.

I marched right out of that lunchroom
full of baffled kids, my fist crammed in
my own mouth, and made my way down to
Pike's Pond, where a particular kind of fish
lives that looks a lot like someone I hate.

Some people say revenge is a dish best served cold. I like to think it's a dish best served pan-seared with diced shallots and a side of ramps.

Thursday
What have I done? It's good that I
avoided punching Marvin and Jones with a
roomful of witnesses. On the other hand,
I also managed to publicly announce my
participation in the science fair. The ABA
has already given me "bookworm" status
and threatened to revoke my membership.

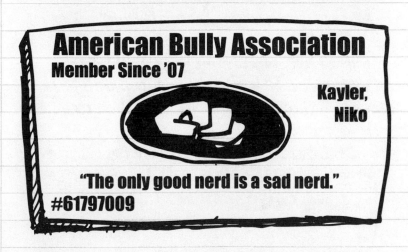

American Bully Association
Member Since '07

Kayler,
Niko

"The only good nerd is a sad nerd."
#61797009

This is why I always say nonviolence
never solved anything.

Friday

After almost being forced to punch the vice principal, I was feeling lower than a puddle of mud, but then I checked my calendar. Did you know that it has been forty days and forty nights since my last official act of schoolyard bullying? That's how long Noah went without bullying! Not to brag, but that's pretty freaking impressive, considering what I've been through in the last couple days. I don't want to jump the gun, but I think I may be cured.

If I just continue to release my bullying urges in a safe and controlled way, outside of school, away from Jones's watchful jerk eye, then everything will be OK.

As long as I stay focused on targets like Alex, Old Man McGee (recently released from the ha-ha house), the late Carlos (yes, I can still bully him from beyond the grave), the fish population of Pike's Pond, and my new next-door neighbor, Mr. Billson, I should be able to behave at school.

I know you don't believe me, Journal, but I have come to control my powers, like a Jedi knight, but way less nerdy.

Now the only question is, what in the world am I going to do about the science fair?

Saturday

Things I would rather do to the science fair
instead of going to it:

1. Blow it up
2. Cover it in licorice and eat it
3. Poke it in the eye with a twig
4. Put it in a stretch limo and drive it
   off a cliff
5. Feed it a salami sandwich on rye, but
   not offer it anything to drink to
   wash it down
6. Pay it a compliment by saying it has nice
   hair, then immediately negate that by
   asking did it do something different
7. Call it racist
8. Just not go to it!

If I can't think of a way out of this by next
week, I might just overdose on candy and soda
so I can stay home.

162

Monday

I'm a genius, a mother-puking genius! I was so worried all weekend about the science fair that I couldn't see that the answer is right in front of me.

Through discipline and creativity, I've managed to turn a vicious junkyard dog of a bully (me) into a model student (at least on the outside). It's a scientific way for bullies to do their thing even in the presence of überjerks like Jones. I call it the NIKO system.

Nice when people are watching
Insist on safe bullying conditions
Keep away bad attention
Opportunity for normal life

By controlling when and how I bully, I can maintain the appearance of being a normal, nonbully student while at the same time releasing my horrific urges to bully in safe and controlled ways. It's perfect for the stupid science fair.

All I need is a test to prove it. I called an emergency meeting with crazy Razey to talk him into trying out the *NIKO* system. The results were exciting.

Boom shaka laka! Or for nerds out there, "The hypothesis holds." When I take this bad boy to the science fair and show that I can successfully rehabilitate hardened criminals using the *NIKO* system, I'll easily take first prize and obliterate the hopes and dreams of a generation of dweebs.

Like I always say, it's not nerdy if the end goal is mischief.

Thursday
Out of the blue today, I got a really weird phone call.

Niko, this is your father, Mr. Kayler. Listen, your mother tells me you finally took some initiative and did something with yourself: You entered the science fair. Anyway, I'll be there to support you.

Support me? I haven't seen the guy in eight months and now he's going to "support me"? What does that even mean? The last time I saw him was when he showed up for my twelfth birthday three days late. The time before that I was staying at his house upstate. He spent all night drinking with his work friends and came home with some lady named "Crystal." She had a ton of tattoos,

including a Chinese character on her lower
back she said meant "chastity." Dad barely
said a word to me before leaving with her,
his breath smelled like the homeless guy's
at the bus station, and I think he even
called me "Miko."

I wonder if it's too late to pull out of
this science fair crap.

Tuesday: The Big Science Fair

I've got good news and bad news. The good news is that I won first place at the science fair. The bad news is that the prize was immediately revoked.

I guess the other bad news is almost everything else that happened.

But let's start from the beginning. There I was, at school at 6:30 in the morning, like a real dingbat. I spent an entire hour setting up my science fair booth in the gym—it had to be perfect. The other projects didn't stand a chance.

The NIKO system dominated. It blew everyone away. I had Vice Principal Jones and all his cronies eating out of my hand. I even arranged for crazy Razey to get a special day pass to the school to help with the science project by doing a live demonstration.

crazy even gave an interview to the school newspaper.

"So, Mr. Razor Blade, can you tell me how the NIKO system has turned you from criminal to cat lover?"

"LIKE NIKO SAYS, ALL I GOTTA DO IS BE NICE WHEN IT COUNTS, INSIST ON SAFE BULLYING CONDITIONS TO KEEP AWAY BAD ATTENTION, AND I GET THE OPPORTUNITY FOR A NORMAL LIFE."

"Amazing. You look so normal now, but are you saying you're still bonkers on the inside?"

"ABSOLUTELY. IN MY MIND'S EYE, MY THOUGHTS LIGHT FIRES IN YOUR CITIES."

"Huh, interesting. . . . Thanks!"

But I couldn't enjoy any of this, because the entire time my eyes were glued to the gym entrances for any sign of my dad. I was getting so nervous that I sweated through my shirt, so crazy gave me his prison shirt. He joked that I should get used to it. Maybe he was right.

Ten minutes before the end of the science fair, I got a call.

"Niko, it's your father, Mr. Kayler. Listen, I'm calling because something came up and I have to cancel on the science fair this afternoon."

"You're not coming?"

"I know you'll understand. But you should call my secretary and have her set up a lunch sometime. I'm pretty busy this month. And next. Ciao."

That phone call was so bad, I am at a loss for words; in fact, I'll just let this unhappy LOLdoggie describe it for me.

it m8 mE sad lik wen me found out der iz no sanTa Clawz

The icing on the cake was that Marvin Rooney happened to overhear.

Oh man, Niko, that really blows. My dad couldn't come today, either, but we'll always have science, right!

Then came the sprinkles on the icing on that cake. (Side note: Getting kinda hungry here.)

I don't know what caused it exactly, but at that moment, something popped inside of my brain. Maybe it was because my dad sucked it up and embarrassed me again, or the fact that Marvin now considered me a nerd buddy of his, or maybe it was Rachel breaking my heart with those five little words. Probably it was a combo of all three. Whatever it was, my months of hard work were about to fall apart. NIKO was about to experience its first systematic failure.

Not thinking, I went into full-on bully mode.

I decided that I would use Marvin as a human domino to set a fire the school wouldn't soon forget. Remember the cage of mice from Fred Peekman's stupid cuteness project? Now I needed a mouse's natural enemy, the spotted barn owl. But since I don't own a spotted barn owl, Marvin would have to do.

A gentle push of the skateboard and the
owl formerly known as Marvin Rooney went
shooting across the gym on a beeline toward
Fred Peekman. Fred of course jumped out
of the way, as I predicted he would, leaving
his cage of mice to meet face-to-face
with their natural enemy.

What do mice do when they're scared?
Like a common nerd, they turn and run. In
this case, they ran right out of the gym into
checkers Nixon Memorial's mascot holding
pen, home to Daisy, the adult African elephant.

Just as the spotted barn owl is the natural
enemy of the mouse, the mouse is in turn the
natural enemy of the adult African elephant.
As I had calculated, the mice gave Daisy such
a fright that she too ran—this time back
toward the gym, which Daisy decided to enter,
but not by using a door.

When the science fair squares saw two tons of pachyderm stampeding toward them, they decided to run, too—this time straight to the gym exit. As they went bursting out the door to "safety," a little

surprise awaited them by the name of Princess smelly.
Moments earlier, right after I gave Marvin his
heave-ho shove, I had placed a call to the Princess,
letting her know that she should come join the party.

Does every good prank have to end with a group of nerds getting bombarded by horrible smells? *No*, but the good ones usually do.

That was the end of the prank, or so I thought, but apparently things went a little further. During the chaos, the *NIKO* system failed again when Crazy Razey saw his opportunity to escape his guards. Leaving out the hole Daisy came in, Crazy used his honed criminal skills to hot-wire and steal Vice Principal Jones's 1991 Dodge Neon. He then went to a Burger Hut, where he ordered a bunch of burgers and a side of cash. Several burgers were harmed in the process.

I think it's safe to say that will be my last science fair at Checkers Nixon Memorial.

Wednesday

Mom took the news of my expulsion better than I thought she would.

After she cooled off, she handed down the sentence: three life terms of consecutive grounding to be served concurrently, without the possibility of pizza. In other words: no fun from now until I die.

Tomorrow, I start my first day at the special school for bad kids: the Lindsay Lohan Academy for Misguided Youths. I am not psyched about it.

Thursday

What is the Lindsay Lohan Academy for
Misguided Youths like? Imagine a prison full
of mental patients on a planet where gravity
doesn't pull your feet to the ground; instead
it pulls people's fists to your face.

I have never met a group of more deranged
bullies in my life. They don't even care about
the art of bullying, only inflicting maximum
damage. I look at bullying as the job of a
crafty sniper who carefully sets up the shot,
waits until the perfect second, and then lets
her rip. These guys at Lohan are like nuclear
bombs. They don't care what or how they bully,
just that somebody is getting hurt.

Today I saw someone get his mouth glued shut! It would have been great if he were a fat guy and they fed him a glue stew or something, but this was just some random act of violence. Worst of all, it was the principal of Lindsay Lohan.

They say on your first day at Lohan you're
supposed to bully someone or make someone
your bully, but I wasn't ready for conflict. So
I kept my head down and managed to figure
out who the key players are.

Kyle Diggs, aka the Trash Compactor

They call Kyle "the Trash Compactor" because
he spends most of his day eating garbage. He
does this to make people think he is crazy
and to give himself such a stink breath that
talking to him will make you faint. He is the
most sane of all the bullies in the school.

Jesus Jimenez, aka the Muscle, aka the Time Bomb

Don't let his name fool you, Jesus is no savior. You know how superfit dudes have six-packs? this guy has a twenty-seven-pack. His muscles have muscles. He spends most of his day lifting iron disks that weigh twice what I do. Word is he hasn't done anything yet but could crack at any moment.

Madison McNulty, aka Mad Madison, aka Mad Madison McNutty

This girl is the most heavily medicated person I know. She has pills to calm her down, pills to wake her up, and other pills the government classifies as experimental. To make herself as crazy as possible, she grinds up all the pills and mixes them together in a Sprite can. She calls this her "crazy soda" and drinks one every day at noon, goes into a trance, and then commits a heinous act of bullying. I heard one time she mailed a kid's shoes to Bulgaria. Not so bad, right? Wrong: His feet were still in them.

Josh Higgins, aka the Adult, aka
Grandpa Josh

The man has grandkids. Josh is twenty-nine
years old and has been at Lindsay Lohan since
it opened in 2001. He's older than most of the
teachers but can't seem to pass seventh grade.
Today I saw a girl ask him how old he was.
Big mistake. His face turned bright red, then
purple, then almost black. A blood vessel burst
in his left eye. He clenched his mouth so tight
that his incisors shattered. Lucky for the
girl, at that moment Principal Adler walked
into Josh's path and absorbed most of the
fallout. On the upside, all the punching loosened
up the glue that was holding Adler's mouth
shut, so I guess it was win-win.

Brittany Flowers, aka Daughter of the Devil, aka The Last Person You Will Ever See

The head honcho at Lohan is the most innocent-looking one of them all. Brittany Flowers has been in and out of every boarding school, reform academy, and juvenile hall there is. She even got thrown out of that Swedish internment camp where they send serial killers who survive the electric chair. From what I gather, there's absolutely no method to her madness. One second she is sweet, adorable Brittany, the next you wake up in a hospital and the doctor tells you you'll never play the piano again, not that you ever could.

Let's just say that my odds don't look good. I don't know how much longer I can keep my head down before these monsters decide to come at me.

Last Will and Testament of Niko Kayler

I, NIKO MARY-SUSAN KAYLER (if
you laugh, you die), being of sound mind,
declare that this is my will.

First: To my beloved friend Carlos I
leave my bedroom, bed, and all my Dr.
MurderGun games. Though he may be
imaginary and dead, Carlos's friendship
was not, and he deserves this stuff.
After all, I'm sure there'll be way more
awesome super violent games for me
to play in hell. I bet the Devil has great
taste in video games.

Second: To my mom I leave my clothes and
photographs of me. I assume she'll need
these to construct a giant shrine in my
honor.

Third: To my little brother, Alex, I leave my remote-controlled truck that he's had his eyes on for years. One stipulation: Truck must only be used in a violent or destructive manner.

Fourth: To my dad I leave my jar of toenail clippings. Whatever.

Fifth: To my dear pet, Princess Smelly, I leave my dear pet Princess Smelly. You're free now, girl, go and explore the world! Spray the Eiffel Tower! Stink up the Seine! The world is your smelly oyster shell.

Last: To the Smithsonian, I leave this journal. Future generations will benefit from my vast knowledge of bullying. Also, they can have whatever is left of my brain after Brittany Flowers finishes digesting it.

Friday
I knew the hit would come, I just didn't
expect so soon.

Day two, 8:00 a.m. First period hadn't
even started when I walked into a
surprisingly silent courtyard. The place
was completely empty save for an ominous
wind blowing across the grass.

Up ahead about fifteen yards sat a
package. Carefully wrapped in Brittany
Flowers's favorite Burberry wrapping
paper, it was obviously a trap—the last
trap I'd ever see.

Mama mia—for real this time.

I took a step backward but felt the hot, trashy breath of Kyle Diggs on my neck. I knew that if I didn't play into their little game and take the beating, I'd receive a much worse punishment later.

The combination of the garbage smell and fear made vomit rise up in my stomach, but I somehow fought it back down. Is this what it feels like to be a nerd?

I did the only thing I could. I marched forward. From the corners of my eyes, I saw the other bullies slowly emerge from the shadows in their war paint. Their quiet murmur grew louder and louder until I could make out the words of the chant "Fish, Fish, Fish!"

Turning to my left, I saw Mad Madison sipping on her crazy soda. I guess she'd made an exception to her noon rule and decided to have one early, for my sake. To my right, Principal Adler hung suspended in some sort of giant spiderweb of chewing gum.

Twenty more steps and I'd be there.
Fifteen. Ten. The "fish" chants were growing
deafening. Five more steps. I was sweating
so bad, my shorts were slipping off me. Just
as I approached the box, I saw what will
haunt my dreams for years to come. To my
right, perched on the edge of the fountain,
was Brittany Flowers. I could tell by the
distant look in her eyes that she was no
longer the cute, adorable Brittany and was
now very much the mayor of Crazy Town. The
chanting stopped.

I was terrified but tried to talk my way out. Maybe if I could convince them I was on their side, they would go easy on me.

"I'm not a nerd. I'm one of you. I'm a madman, a sociopath! I have a pet skunk and am friends with a criminal named Razor Blade. I hate nerds—I eat them for breakfast."

"Silence!" Brittany barked. "In here, you are the nerd."

Like clockwork, the chanting started up again. Brittany motioned toward the package. Three more steps and I held in my hands what was surely some kind of IED made of Legos and thumbtacks. I closed my eyes and opened it, but nothing exploded.

Was that it? All this hoopla just to make me eat a worm? I eat worms for fun (it's a great way to gross out girls). Maybe I had given these "bullies" too much credit. I happily downed the worm, and the chanting stopped once again. Then I smelled the all too familiar smell of garbage breath rise up from under me.

With that cryptic remark, I was thrown
into the fountain. Again, I thought I'd
escaped until I emerged soaked and glanced
up to see Jesus and Josh at the edge of the
fountain.

Have you ever been bitten by two hundred
bloodthirsty fish at the same time? On the
fun scale, it ranks somewhere between a
triple root canal and being forced to eat the
cutest puppy in the world using only a spoon.

Sunday

I woke up in the school nurse's office. It took three hours to remove all the piranhas from my body, most of which had clustered around my butt.

What they did to me was horrible. I was violated and degraded. I felt the full force of bully bearing down on me: I was the nerd. They took something away from me that I can never get back. I can't believe I used to do this to other people. What was I thinking? What kind of monster was I? Can I ever right the wrongs of my past? I will do anything and everything in my power so that I never make others feel the way I did that day.

At least that's what I told Mom and Dr. Shaeffer.

In reality, I feel quite the opposite. What didn't kill me has only made me stronger. These bullies are going to pay, and they're going to pay **hard**. One by one I am going to teach these bullies—_these amateurs_—what it means to be a real bully. Soon they'll be down on their knees, begging me for mercy. Before I'm done here, they will look upon me with fear and call me "Daddy."

About the Author

Farley Katz is a cartoonist and writer from Texas who lives in New York where he draws for the _New Yorker_. check out FarleyKatz.com for more info.